ROSEMARY WELLS
TIMOTHY GOES TO SCHOOL

VIKING

VIKING
Published by the Penguin Group
Penguin Putnam Books for Young Readers, 345 Hudson Street, New York, New York 10014, U.S.A.
Penguin Books Ltd, 27 Wrights Lane, London W8 5TZ, England
Penguin Books Australia Ltd, Ringwood, Victoria, Australia
Penguin Books Canada Ltd, 10 Alcorn Avenue, Toronto, Ontario, Canada M4V 3B2
Penguin Books (N.Z.) Ltd, 182-190 Wairau Road, Auckland 10, New Zealand

Penguin Books Ltd, Registered Offices: Harmondsworth, Middlesex, England

First published in 1981 by Dial Books for Young Readers, a member of Penguin Putnam Inc.

Published with new illustrations in 2000 by Viking, a division of Penguin Putnam
Books for Young Readers.

10   9   8   7   6   5

The Library of Congress has catalogued the Dial edition as follows:
Wells, Rosemary / Timothy goes to school.
Summary: Timothy learns about being accepted and making friends during the first week
of his first year at school.
[1. School stories] I. Title.
PZ7.W46843Ti [E]   80-20785
ISBN 0-8037-8948-3 / ISBN 0-8037-8949-1 (lib. bdg.)

Viking ISBN 0-670-89182-7

Printed in Hong Kong
Set in Minister

The art for this book was prepared in the usual way: with watercolor, pen and ink,
gouache, pastel, and rubber stamps.

For Mimi Kayden

TIMOTHY'S mother made him a brand-new sunsuit for the first day of school.

"Hooray!" said Timothy.

Timothy went to school in his new sunsuit
with his new book and his new pencil.

"Good morning!" said Timothy.
"Good morning!" said Mrs. Jenkins.

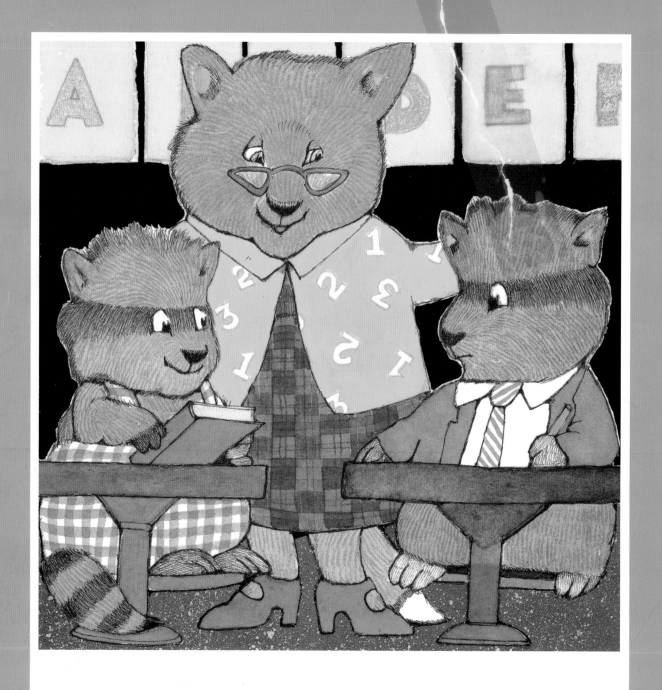

"Timothy," said Mrs. Jenkins, "this is
Claude. Claude, this is Timothy. I'm sure
you'll be the best of friends."

A B C D E F G H

"Hello!" said Timothy.
"Nobody wears a sunsuit on the first day of school," said Claude.

During playtime Timothy hoped and
hoped that Claude would fall into a puddle.

But he didn't.

When Timothy came home, his mother asked,
"How was school today?"

"Nobody wears a sunsuit on the first day of
school," said Timothy.

"I will make you a beautiful new jacket,"
said Timothy's mother.

Timothy wore his new jacket the next day.

"Hello!" said Timothy to Claude.
"You're not supposed to wear party clothes
on the second day of school," said Claude.

All day Timothy wanted and wanted Claude
to make a mistake.

But he didn't.

When Timothy went home, his mother asked,
"How did it go?"

"You're not supposed to wear party clothes
on the second day of school," said Timothy.
"Don't worry," said Timothy's mother.
"Tomorrow you just wear something in-between
like everyone else."

The next day Timothy went to school in his favorite shirt.

"Look!" said Timothy. "You are wearing the same shirt I am!"

"No," said Claude, "*you* are wearing the same shirt that *I* am."

During lunch Timothy wished and wished
that Claude would have to eat all alone.

But he didn't.

After school Timothy's mother could not find
Timothy. "Where are you?" she called.
   "I'm never going back to school," said Timothy.
   "Why not?" called his mother.

"Because Claude is the smartest and the best at everything and he has all the friends," said Timothy.

"You'll feel better in your new football shirt," said Timothy's mother.

Timothy did not feel better in his new
football shirt.

That morning Claude played the saxophone.
"I can't stand it anymore," said a voice next to
Timothy.

It was Violet.

"You can't stand what?" Timothy asked Violet.

"Grace!" said Violet. "She sings. She dances. She counts up to a thousand and she sits next to me!"

During playtime Timothy and Violet
stayed together.

Violet said, "I can't believe you've been here all along!"

"Will you come home and have cookies with me after school?" Timothy asked.

On the way home Timothy and Violet laughed
so much about Claude and Grace that they both
got the hiccups.